Crab Cakes

Kelly Doudna

Illustrated by Anne Haberstroh

Consulting Editor, Diane Craig, M.A./Reading Specialist

Published by ABDO Publishing Company, 4940 Viking Drive, Edina, Minnesota 55435.

Printed in the United States.

Credits
Edited by: Pam Price
Curriculum Coordinator: Nancy Tuminelly
Cover and Interior Design and Production: Mighty Media
Photo Credits: Corel, iStockphoto/Hatem El-Toudy, iStockphoto/David Hanson, iStockphoto/Dragan Trifunovic, Photodisc, ShutterStock

Library of Congress Cataloging-in-Publication Data

Doudna, Kelly, 1963-
    Crab cakes / Kelly Doudna; illustrated by Anne Haberstroh.
        p. cm. -- (Fact & fiction. Critter chronicles)
    Summary: Sandy Crab enjoys the festivities at her wedding reception. Alternating pages provide facts about crabs.
    ISBN 10 1-59928-434-0 (hardcover)
    ISBN 10 1-59928-435-9 (paperback)

    ISBN 13 978-1-59928-434-7 (hardcover)
    ISBN 13 978-1-59928-435-4 (paperback)
    [1. Weddings--Fiction. 2. Crabs--Fiction.] I. Haberstroh, Anne, ill. II. Title. III. Series.

PZ7.D74425Cr 2006
[E]--dc22

                                                                                    2006005539

SandCastle Level: Fluent

SandCastle™ books are created by a professional team of educators, reading specialists, and content developers around five essential components—phonemic awareness, phonics, vocabulary, text comprehension, and fluency—to assist young readers as they develop reading skills and strategies and increase their general knowledge. All books are written, reviewed, and leveled for guided reading, early reading intervention, and Accelerated Reader® programs for use in shared, guided, and independent reading and writing activities to support a balanced approach to literacy instruction. The SandCastle™ series has four levels that correspond to early literacy development. The levels help teachers and parents select appropriate books for young readers.

Emerging Readers   **Beginning Readers**   **Transitional Readers**   **Fluent Readers**
(no flags)   (1 flag)   (2 flags)   (3 flags)

These levels are meant only as a guide. All levels are subject to change.

FACT & FiCTiON

This series provides early fluent readers the opportunity to develop reading comprehension strategies and increase fluency. These books are appropriate for guided, shared, and independent reading.

FACT The left-hand pages incorporate realistic photographs to enhance readers' understanding of informational text.

FiCTiON The right-hand pages engage readers with an entertaining, narrative story that is supported by whimsical illustrations.

The Fact and Fiction pages can be read separately to improve comprehension through questioning, predicting, making inferences, and summarizing. They can also be read side-by-side, in spreads, which encourages students to explore and examine different writing styles.

FACT OR **FiCTiON?** This fun quiz helps reinforce students' understanding of what is real and not real.

SPEED READ The text-only version of each section includes word-count rulers for fluency practice and assessment.

GLOSSARY Higher-level vocabulary and concepts are defined in the glossary.

SandCastle™ would like to hear from you.

Tell us your stories about reading this book. What was your favorite page? Was there something hard that you needed help with? Share the ups and downs of learning to read. To get posted on the ABDO Publishing Company Web site, send us an e-mail at:

sandcastle@abdopublishing.com

Crabs are decapods. That means they have ten legs. The front pair of legs has developed into claws.

Sandy Crab has just gotten married, and the guests are dancing at the reception. Sandy shouts, "Come on, everyone! Let's start a conga line!" Everybody marches around, kicking their legs every few steps.

5

Male crabs will often wave their large claws in the air to attract females or to scare off other males.

The band has everyone tapping their toes and waving their claws as they wind around the room. Sandy grabs a cowbell and bangs on it.

The legs on one side of a crab's body pull the crab along while the legs on the other side push. This creates the sideways walk that crabs are famous for.

"This is fun, but I'm out
of breath!" Sandy gasps.
She slides sideways into a
chair at a table next to her
Uncle Joe and takes a big drink
of fruit punch.

9

Crabs have small, leglike mouthparts to hold and chew food.

Sandy cuts the wedding cake.
She asks, "Uncle Joe, would you
like a piece of cake?"

"I'll have two, please!" he replies.

11

Crabs are scavengers. They will eat
whatever they can find, whether it's plants
or other creatures.

Uncle Joe eats not only the
cake but everything else in sight.

"Uncle Joe, there won't be anything
left for anyone else to eat!" Sandy
exclaims.

13

Crabs have two compound eyes that sit at the ends of short eyestalks. Crabs see quite well.

Sandy looks around the room and sees her mother sitting to the side, crying. "Mom, what's the matter?" Sandy asks.

"I'm just so happy!" Mrs. Crab weeps, dabbing at her eyestalks with a tissue. "My little crab is all grown up."

Fiction

15

Crabs are crustaceans and must molt in order to grow. Each time a crab sheds its shell, the crab grows a little larger.

Mrs. Crab takes
out a fresh tissue.
"Sandy, you look
so beautiful in that
dress!" she cries.

"Thanks, Mom, but I can't wait to change into
something more comfortable!" Sandy declares.

17

Some crabs live mostly on land. Other crabs live mostly in the water and are called swimming crabs.

At the end of the
evening, Sandy hugs
Mrs. Crab and says,
"Time for me to be off on my
honeymoon, two weeks of fun
in the sand and surf. I'll send
you a postcard!"

19

FACT or Fiction?

Read each statement below. Then decide whether it's from the FACT section or the Fiction section!

  1. Crabs get married.

  2. Crabs dance in conga lines.

 3. Crabs see quite well.

 4. Crabs must molt in order to grow.

Crabs are decapods. That means they have ten legs. 9
The front pair of legs has developed into claws. 18

Male crabs will often wave their large claws in the 28
air to attract females or to scare off other males. 38

The legs on one side of a crab's body pull the crab 50
along while the legs on the other side push. This 60
creates the sideways walk that crabs are famous for. 69

Crabs have small, leglike mouthparts to hold and 77
chew food. 79

Crabs are scavengers. They will eat whatever they 87
can find, whether it's plants or other creatures. 95

Crabs have two compound eyes that sit at the ends 105
of short eyestalks. Crabs see quite well. 112

Crabs are crustaceans and must molt in order to 121
grow. Each time a crab sheds its shell, the crab grows a 133
little larger. 135

Some crabs live mostly on land. Other crabs live 144
mostly in the water and are called swimming crabs. 153

21

Sandy Crab has just gotten married, and the guests are dancing at the reception. Sandy shouts, "Come on, everyone! Let's start a conga line!" Everybody marches around, kicking their legs every few steps.

The band has everyone tapping their toes and waving their claws as they wind around the room. Sandy grabs a cowbell and bangs on it.

"This is fun, but I'm out of breath!" Sandy gasps. She slides sideways into a chair at a table next to her Uncle Joe and takes a big drink of fruit punch.

Sandy cuts the wedding cake. She asks, "Uncle Joe, would you like a piece of cake?"

"I'll have two, please!" he replies.

Uncle Joe eats not only the cake but everything else in sight.

"Uncle Joe, there won't be anything left for anyone else to eat!" Sandy exclaims.

8
15
23
29
33
41
49
58
67
77
88
90
98
106
112
120
124
132
138

Sandy looks around the room and sees her 146
mother sitting to the side, crying. "Mom, what's the 155
matter?" Sandy asks. 158

"I'm just so happy!" Mrs. Crab weeps, dabbing at 167
her eyestalks with a tissue. "My little crab is all 177
grown up." 179

Mrs. Crab takes out a fresh tissue. "Sandy, you 188
look so beautiful in that dress!" she cries. 196

"Thanks, Mom, but I can't wait to change into 205
something more comfortable!" Sandy declares. 210

At the end of the evening, Sandy hugs Mrs. Crab 220
and says, "Time for me to be off on my 230
honeymoon, two weeks of fun in the sand and surf. 240
I'll send you a postcard!" 245

GLOSSARY

compound eye. an eye that is made up of many separate visual units

crustacean. a sea creature, such as a lobster, crab, or shrimp, that has a hard, external skeleton

honeymoon. a trip taken by a newly married couple

molt. to periodically shed feathers, fur, or another outer covering

mouthpart. a part of the body near the mouth adapted for use in gathering or eating food

scavenger. one that feeds on whatever garbage or dead animals it finds

surf. ocean waves as they hit the shore

To see a complete list of SandCastle™ books and other nonfiction titles from ABDO Publishing Company, visit www.abdopublishing.com or contact us at: 4940 Viking Drive, Edina, Minnesota 55435 • 1-800-800-1312 • fax: 1-952-831-1632